AS A MAN THINKE

BY

JAMES ALLEN

Author of "From Passion to Peace"

Mind is the Master power that moulds and makes,
And Man is Mind, and evermore he takes
The tool of Thought, and, shaping what he wills,
Brings forth a thousand joys, a thousand ills:—
He thinks in secret, and it comes to pass:
Environment is but his looking-glass.

Authorized Edition

New York

CONTENTS

FOREWORD

THIS little volume (the result of meditation and experience) is not intended as an exhaustive treatise on the much-written-upon subject of the power of thought. It is suggestive rather than explanatory, its object being to stimulate men and women to the discovery and perception of the truth that—

"They themselves are makers of themselves."

by virtue of the thoughts, which they choose and encourage; that mind is the master-weaver, both of the inner garment of character and the outer garment of circumstance, and that, as they may have hitherto woven in ignorance and pain they may now weave in enlightenment and happiness.

JAMES ALLEN.

BROAD PARK AVENUE,

ILFRACOMBE,

ENGLAND

THOUGHT AND CHARACTER

THE aphorism, "As a man thinketh in his heart so is he," not only embraces the whole of a man's being, but is so comprehensive as to reach out to every condition and circumstance of his life. A man is literally what he thinks, his character being the complete sum of all his thoughts.

As the plant springs from, and could not be without, the seed, so every act of a man springs from the hidden seeds of thought, and could not have appeared without them. This applies equally to those acts called "spontaneous" and "unpremeditated" as to those, which are deliberately executed.

Act is the blossom of thought, and joy and suffering are its fruits; thus does a man garner in the sweet and bitter fruitage of his own husbandry.

"Thought in the mind hath made us, What we are
By thought was wrought and built. If a man's mind
Hath evil thoughts, pain comes on him as comes
The wheel the ox behind....
..If one endure
In purity of thought, joy follows him
As his own shadow—sure."

Man is a growth by law, a3nd not a creation by artifice, and cause and effect is as absolute and undeviating in the hidden realm of thought as in the world of visible and material things. A noble and Godlike character is not a thing of favour or chance, but is the natural result of continued effort in right thinking, the effect of long-cherished association with Godlike thoughts. An ignoble and bestial character, by the same process, is the result of the continued harbouring of grovelling thoughts.

Man is made or unmade by himself; in the armoury of thought he forges the weapons by which he destroys himself; he also fashions the tools with which he builds for himself heavenly mansions of joy and strength and peace. By the right choice and true application of thought, man ascends to the Divine Perfection; by the abuse and wrong application of thought, he descends below the level of the beast. Between these two extremes are all the grades of character, and man is their maker and master.

Of all the beautiful truths pertaining to the soul which have been restored and brought to light in this age, none is more gladdening or fruitful of divine promise and confidence than this—that man is the master of thought, the moulder of character, and the maker and shaper of condition, environment, and destiny.

As a being of Power, Intelligence, and Love, and the lord of his own thoughts, man holds the key to every situation, and contains within himself that transforming and regenerative agency by which he may make himself what he wills.

Man is always the master, even in his weaker and most abandoned state; but in his weakness and degradation he is the foolish master who misgoverns his "household." When he begins to reflect upon his condition, and to search diligently for the Law upon which his being is established, he then becomes the wise master, directing his energies with intelligence, and fashioning his thoughts to fruitful issues. Such is the conscious master, and man can only thus become by discovering within himself the laws of thought; which discovery is totally a matter of application, self analysis, and experience.

Only by much searching and mining, are gold and diamonds obtained, and man can find every truth connected with his being, if he will dig deep into the mine of his soul; and that he is the maker of his character, the moulder of his life, and the builder of his destiny, he may unerringly prove, if he will watch, control, and alter his thoughts, tracing their effects upon himself, upon others, and upon his life and circumstances, linking cause and effect by patient practice and investigation, and utilizing his every experience, even to the most trivial, everyday occurrence, as a means of obtaining that knowledge of himself which is Understanding, Wisdom, Power. In this direction, as in no other, is the law absolute that "He that seeketh findeth; and to him that knocketh it shall be opened;" for only by patience, practice, and ceaseless importunity can a man enter the Door of the Temple of Knowledge.

EFFECT OF THOUGHT ON CIRCUMSTANCES

MAN'S mind may be likened to a garden, which may be intelligently cultivated or allowed to run wild; but whether cultivated or neglected, it must, and will, bring forth. If no useful seeds are put into it, then an abundance of useless weed-seeds will fall therein, and will continue to produce their kind.

Just as a gardener cultivates his plot, keeping it free from weeds, and growing the flowers and fruits which he requires, so may a man tend the garden of his mind, weeding out all the wrong, useless, and impure thoughts, and cultivating toward perfection the flowers and fruits of right, useful, and pure thoughts. By pursuing this process, a man sooner or later discovers that he is the master-gardener of his soul, the director of his life. He also reveals, within himself, the laws of thought, and understands, with ever-increasing accuracy, how the thought-forces and mind elements operate in the shaping of his character, circumstances, and destiny.

Thought and character are one, and as character can only manifest and discover itself through environment and circumstance, the outer conditions of a person's life will always be found to be harmoniously related to his inner state. This does not mean that a man's circumstances at any given time are an indication of his entire character, but that those circumstances are so intimately connected with some vital thought-element within himself that, for the time being, they are indispensable to his development.

Every man is where he is by the law of his being; the thoughts which he has built into his character have brought him there, and in the arrangement of his life there is no element of chance, but all is the result of a law which cannot err. This is just as true of those who feel "out of harmony" with their surroundings as of those who are contented with them.

As a progressive and evolving being, man is where he is that he may learn that he may grow; and as he learns the spiritual lesson which any circumstance contains for him, it passes away and gives place to other circumstances.

Man is buffeted by circumstances so long as he believes himself to be the creature of outside conditions, but when he realizes that he is a creative power, and that he may command the hidden soil and seeds of his being out of which circumstances grow, he then becomes the rightful master of himself.

That circumstances grow out of thought every man knows who has for any length of time practised self-control and self-purification, for he will have noticed that the alteration in his circumstances has been in exact ratio with his altered mental condition. So true is this that when a man earnestly applies himself to remedy the defects in his character, and makes swift and marked progress, he passes rapidly through a succession of vicissitudes.

The soul attracts that which it secretly harbours; that which it loves, and also that which it fears; it reaches the height of its cherished aspirations; it falls to the level of its unchastened desires,—and circumstances are the means by which the soul receives its own.

Every thought-seed sown or allowed to fall into the mind, and to take root there, produces its own, blossoming sooner or later into act, and bearing its own fruitage of opportunity and circumstance. Good thoughts bear good fruit, bad thoughts bad fruit.

The outer world of circumstance shapes itself to the inner world of thought, and both pleasant and unpleasant external conditions are factors, which make for the ultimate good of the individual. As the reaper of his own harvest, man learns both by suffering and bliss.

Following the inmost desires, aspirations, thoughts, by which he allows himself to be dominated, (pursuing the will-o'-the-wisps of impure imaginings or steadfastly walking the highway of strong and high endeavour), a man at last arrives at their fruition and fulfilment in the outer conditions of his life. The laws of growth and adjustment everywhere obtains.

A man does not come to the almshouse or the jail by the tyranny of fate or circumstance, but by the pathway of grovelling thoughts and base desires. Nor does a pure-minded man fall suddenly into crime by stress of any mere external force; the criminal thought had long been secretly fostered in the heart, and the hour of opportunity revealed its gathered power. Circumstance does not make the man; it reveals him to himself. No such conditions can exist as descending into vice and its attendant sufferings apart from vicious inclinations, or ascending into virtue and its pure happiness without the continued cultivation of virtuous aspirations; and man, therefore, as the lord and master of thought, is the maker of himself the shaper and author of environment. Even at birth the soul comes to its own and through every step of its earthly pilgrimage it attracts those combinations of conditions which reveal itself, which are the reflections of its own purity and, impurity, its strength and weakness.

Men do not attract that which they want, but that which they are. Their whims, fancies, and ambitions are thwarted at every step, but their inmost thoughts and desires are fed with their own food, be it foul or clean. The "divinity that shapes our ends" is in ourselves; it is our very self. Only himself manacles man: thought and action are the gaolers of Fate—they imprison, being base; they are also the angels of Freedom—they liberate, being noble. Not what he wishes and prays for does a man get, but what he justly earns. His wishes and prayers are only gratified and answered when they harmonize with his thoughts and actions.

In the light of this truth, what, then, is the meaning of "fighting against circumstances?" It means that a man is continually revolting against an effect without, while all the time he is nourishing and preserving its cause in his heart. That cause may take the form of a conscious vice or an unconscious weakness; but whatever it is, it stubbornly retards the efforts of its possessor, and thus calls aloud for remedy.

Men are anxious to improve their circumstances, but are unwilling to improve themselves; they therefore remain bound. The man who does not shrink from self-crucifixion can never fail to accomplish the object upon which his heart is set. This is as true of earthly as of heavenly things. Even the man whose sole object is to acquire wealth must be prepared to make great personal sacrifices before he can accomplish his object; and how much more so he who would realize a strong and well-poised life?

Here is a man who is wretchedly poor. He is extremely anxious that his surroundings and home comforts should be improved, yet all the time he shirks his work, and considers he is justified in trying to deceive his employer on the ground of the insufficiency of his wages. Such a man does not understand the simplest rudiments of those principles which are the basis of true prosperity, and is not only totally unfitted to rise out of his wretchedness, but is actually attracting to himself a still deeper wretchedness by dwelling in, and acting out, indolent, deceptive, and unmanly thoughts.

Here is a rich man who is the victim of a painful and persistent disease as the result of gluttony. He is willing to give large sums of money to get rid of it, but he will not sacrifice his gluttonous desires. He wants to gratify his taste for rich and unnatural viands and have his health as well. Such a man is totally unfit to have health, because he has not yet learned the first principles of a healthy life.

Here is an employer of labour who adopts crooked measures to avoid paying the regulation wage, and, in the hope of making larger profits, reduces the wages of his workpeople. Such a man is altogether unfitted for prosperity, and when he finds himself bankrupt, both as regards reputation and riches, he blames circumstances, not knowing that he is the sole author of his condition.

I have introduced these three cases merely as illustrative of the truth that man is the causer (though nearly always is unconsciously) of his circumstances, and that, whilst aiming at a good end, he is continually frustrating its accomplishment by encouraging thoughts and desires which cannot possibly harmonize with that end. Such cases could be multiplied and varied almost indefinitely, but this is not necessary, as the reader can, if he so resolves, trace the action of the laws of thought in his own mind and life, and until this is done, mere external facts cannot serve as a ground of reasoning.

Circumstances, however, are so complicated, thought is so deeply rooted, and the conditions of happiness vary so, vastly with individuals, that a man's entire soul-condition (although it may be known to himself) cannot be judged by another from the external aspect of his life alone. A man may be honest in certain directions, yet suffer privations; a man may be dishonest in certain directions, yet acquire wealth; but the conclusion usually formed that the one man fails because of his particular honesty, and that the other prospers because of his particular dishonesty, is the result of a superficial judgment, which assumes that the dishonest man is almost totally corrupt, and the honest man almost entirely virtuous. In the light of a deeper knowledge and wider experience such judgment is found to be erroneous. The dishonest man may have some admirable virtues, which the other does, not possess; and the honest man obnoxious vices which are absent in the other. The honest man reaps the good results of his honest thoughts and acts; he also brings upon himself the sufferings, which his vices produce. The dishonest man likewise garners his own suffering and happiness.

It is pleasing to human vanity to believe that one suffers because of one's virtue; but not until a man has extirpated every sickly, bitter, and impure thought from his mind, and washed every sinful stain from his soul, can he be in a position to know and declare that his sufferings are the result of his good, and not of his bad qualities; and on the way to, yet long before he has reached, that supreme perfection, he will have found, working in his mind and life, the Great Law which is absolutely just, and which cannot, therefore, give good for evil, evil for good. Possessed of such knowledge, he will then know, looking back upon his past ignorance and blindness, that his life is, and always was, justly ordered, and that all his past experiences, good and bad, were the equitable outworking of his evolving, yet unevolved self.

Good thoughts and actions can never produce bad results; bad thoughts and actions can never produce good results. This is but saying that nothing can come from corn but corn, nothing from nettles but nettles. Men understand this law in the natural world, and work with it; but few understand it in the mental and moral world (though its operation there is just as simple and undeviating), and they, therefore, do not co-operate with it.

Suffering is always the effect of wrong thought in some direction. It is an indication that the individual is out of harmony with himself, with the Law of his being. The sole and supreme use of suffering is to purify, to burn out all that is useless and impure. Suffering ceases for him who is pure. There could be no object in burning gold after the dross had been removed, and a perfectly pure and enlightened being could not suffer.

The circumstances, which a man encounters with suffering, are the result of his own mental in harmony. The circumstances, which a man encounters with blessedness, are the result of his own mental harmony. Blessedness, not material possessions, is the measure of right thought; wretchedness, not lack of material possessions, is the measure of wrong thought. A man may be cursed and rich; he may be blessed and poor. Blessedness and riches are only joined together when the riches are rightly and wisely used; and the poor man only descends into wretchedness when he regards his lot as a burden unjustly imposed.

Indigence and indulgence are the two extremes of wretchedness. They are both equally unnatural and the result of mental disorder. A man is not rightly conditioned until he is a happy, healthy, and prosperous being; and happiness, health, and prosperity are the result of a harmonious adjustment of the inner with the outer, of the man with his surroundings.

A man only begins to be a man when he ceases to whine and revile, and commences to search for the hidden justice which regulates his life. And as he adapts his mind to that regulating factor, he ceases to accuse others as the cause of his condition, and builds himself up in strong and noble thoughts; ceases to kick against circumstances, but begins to use them as aids to his more rapid progress, and as a means of discovering the hidden powers and possibilities within himself.

Law, not confusion, is the dominating principle in the universe; justice, not injustice, is the soul and substance of life; and righteousness, not corruption, is the moulding and moving force in the spiritual government of the world. This being so, man has but to right himself to find that the universe is right; and during the process of putting himself right he will find that as he alters his thoughts towards things and other people, things and other people will alter towards him.

The proof of this truth is in every person, and it therefore admits of easy investigation by systematic introspection and self-analysis. Let a man radically alter his thoughts, and he will be astonished at the rapid transformation it will effect in the material conditions of his life. Men imagine that thought can be kept secret, but it cannot; it rapidly crystallizes into habit, and habit solidifies into circumstance. Bestial thoughts crystallize into habits of drunkenness and sensuality, which solidify into circumstances of destitution and disease: impure thoughts of every kind crystallize into enervating and confusing habits, which solidify into distracting and adverse circumstances: thoughts of fear, doubt, and indecision crystallize into weak, unmanly, and irresolute habits, which solidify into circumstances of failure, indigence, and slavish dependence: lazy thoughts crystallize into habits of uncleanliness and dishonesty, which solidify into circumstances of foulness and beggary: hateful and condemnatory thoughts crystallize into habits of accusation and violence, which solidify into circumstances of injury and persecution: selfish thoughts of all kinds crystallize into habits of self-seeking, which solidify into circumstances more or less distressing. On the other hand, beautiful thoughts of all kinds crystallize into habits of grace and kindliness, which solidify into genial and sunny circumstances: pure thoughts crystallize into habits of temperance and self-control, which solidify into circumstances of repose and peace: thoughts of courage, self-reliance, and decision crystallize into manly habits, which solidify into circumstances of success, plenty, and freedom: energetic thoughts crystallize into habits of cleanliness and industry, which solidify into circumstances of pleasantness: gentle and forgiving thoughts crystallize into habits of gentleness, which solidify into protective and preservative circumstances: loving and unselfish thoughts crystallize into habits of self-forgetfulness for others, which solidify into circumstances of sure and abiding prosperity and true riches.

A particular train of thought persisted in, be it good or bad, cannot fail to produce its results on the character and circumstances. A man cannot directly choose his circumstances, but he can choose his thoughts, and so indirectly, yet surely, shape his circumstances.

Nature helps every man to the gratification of the thoughts, which he most encourages, and opportunities are presented which will most speedily bring to the surface both the good and evil thoughts.

Let a man cease from his sinful thoughts, and all the world will soften towards him, and be ready to help him; let him put away his weakly and sickly thoughts, and lo, opportunities will spring up on every hand to aid his strong resolves; let him encourage good thoughts, and no hard fate shall bind him down to wretchedness and shame. The world is your kaleidoscope, and the varying combinations of colours, which at every succeeding moment it presents to you are the exquisitely adjusted pictures of your ever-moving thoughts.

"So You will be what you will to be;
Let failure find its false content
In that poor word, 'environment,'
But spirit scorns it, and is free.
"It masters time, it conquers space;
It cowes that boastful trickster, Chance,
And bids the tyrant Circumstance
Uncrown, and fill a servant's place.
"The human Will, that force unseen,
The offspring of a deathless Soul,
Can hew a way to any goal,
Though walls of granite intervene.
"Be not impatient in delays
But wait as one who understands;
When spirit rises and commands
The gods are ready to obey."

EFFECT OF THOUGHT ON HEALTH AND THE BODY

THE body is the servant of the mind. It obeys the operations of the mind, whether they be deliberately chosen or automatically expressed. At the bidding of unlawful thoughts the body sinks rapidly into disease and decay; at the command of glad and beautiful thoughts it becomes clothed with youthfulness and beauty.

Disease and health, like circumstances, are rooted in thought. Sickly thoughts will express themselves through a sickly body. Thoughts of fear have been known to kill a man as speedily as a bullet, and they are continually killing thousands of people just as surely though less rapidly. The people who live in fear of disease are the people who get it. Anxiety quickly demoralizes the whole body, and lays it open to the entrance of disease; while impure thoughts, even if not physically indulged, will soon shatter the nervous system.

Strong, pure, and happy thoughts build up the body in vigour and grace. The body is a delicate and plastic instrument, which responds readily to the thoughts by which it is impressed, and habits of thought will produce their own effects, good or bad, upon it.

Men will continue to have impure and poisoned blood, so long as they propagate unclean thoughts. Out of a clean heart comes a clean life and a clean body. Out of a defiled mind proceeds a defiled life and a corrupt body. Thought is the fount of action, life, and manifestation; make the fountain pure, and all will be pure.

Change of diet will not help a man who will not change his thoughts. When a man makes his thoughts pure, he no longer desires impure food.

Clean thoughts make clean habits. The so-called saint who does not wash his body is not a saint. He who has strengthened and purified his thoughts does not need to consider the malevolent microbe.

If you would protect your body, guard your mind. If you would renew your body, beautify your mind. Thoughts of malice, envy, disappointment, despondency, rob the body of its health and grace. A sour face does not come by chance; it is made by sour thoughts. Wrinkles that mar are drawn by folly, passion, and pride.

I know a woman of ninety-six who has the bright, innocent face of a girl. I know a man well under middle age whose face is drawn into inharmonious contours. The one is the result of a sweet and sunny disposition; the other is the outcome of passion and discontent.

As you cannot have a sweet and wholesome abode unless you admit the air and sunshine freely into your rooms, so a strong body and a bright, happy, or serene countenance can only result from the free admittance into the mind of thoughts of joy and goodwill and serenity.

On the faces of the aged there are wrinkles made by sympathy, others by strong and pure thought, and others are carved by passion: who cannot distinguish them? With those who have lived righteously, age is calm, peaceful, and softly mellowed, like the setting sun. I have recently seen a philosopher on his deathbed. He was not old except in years. He died as sweetly and peacefully as he had lived.

There is no physician like cheerful thought for dissipating the ills of the body; there is no comforter to compare with goodwill for dispersing the shadows of grief and sorrow. To live continually in thoughts of ill will, cynicism, suspicion, and envy, is to be confined in a self made prison-hole. But to think well of all, to be cheerful with all, to patiently learn to find the good in all—such unselfish thoughts are the very portals of heaven; and to dwell day by day in thoughts of peace toward every creature will bring abounding peace to their possessor.

THOUGHT AND PURPOSE

UNTIL thought is linked with purpose there is no intelligent accomplishment. With the majority the bark of thought is allowed to "drift" upon the ocean of life. Aimlessness is a vice, and such drifting must not continue for him who would steer clear of catastrophe and destruction.

They who have no central purpose in their life fall an easy prey to petty worries, fears, troubles, and self-pityings, all of which are indications of weakness, which lead, just as surely as deliberately planned sins (though by a different route), to failure, unhappiness, and loss, for weakness cannot persist in a power evolving universe.

A man should conceive of a legitimate purpose in his heart, and set out to accomplish it. He should make this purpose the centralizing point of his thoughts. It may take the form of a spiritual ideal, or it may be a worldly object, according to his nature at the time being; but whichever it is, he should steadily focus his thought-forces upon the object, which he has set before him. He should make this purpose his supreme duty, and should devote himself to its attainment, not allowing his thoughts to wander away into ephemeral fancies, longings, and imaginings. This is the royal road to self-control and true concentration of thought. Even if he fails again and again to accomplish his purpose (as he necessarily must until weakness is overcome), the strength of character gained will be the measure of his true success, and this will form a new starting-point for future power and triumph.

Those who are not prepared for the apprehension of a great purpose should fix the thoughts upon the faultless performance of their duty, no matter how insignificant their task may appear. Only in this way can the thoughts be gathered and focussed, and resolution and energy be developed, which being done, there is nothing which may not be accomplished.

The weakest soul, knowing its own weakness, and believing this truth that strength can only be developed by effort and practice, will, thus believing, at once begin to exert itself, and, adding effort to effort, patience to patience, and strength to strength, will never cease to develop, and will at last grow divinely strong.

As the physically weak man can make himself strong by careful and patient training, so the man of weak thoughts can make them strong by exercising himself in right thinking.

To put away aimlessness and weakness, and to begin to think with purpose, is to enter the ranks of those strong ones who only recognize failure as one of the pathways to attainment; who make all conditions serve them, and who think strongly, attempt fearlessly, and accomplish masterfully.

Having conceived of his purpose, a man should mentally mark out a straight pathway to its achievement, looking neither to the right nor the left. Doubts and fears should be rigorously excluded; they are disintegrating elements, which break up the straight line of effort, rendering it crooked, ineffectual, useless. Thoughts of doubt and fear never accomplished anything, and never can. They always lead to failure. Purpose, energy, power to do, and all strong thoughts cease when doubt and fear creep in.

The will to do springs from the knowledge that we can do. Doubt and fear are the great enemies of knowledge, and he who encourages them, who does not slay them, thwarts himself at every step.

He who has conquered doubt and fear has conquered failure. His every thought is allied with power, and all difficulties are bravely met and wisely overcome. His purposes are seasonably planted, and they bloom and bring forth fruit, which does not fall prematurely to the ground.

Thought allied fearlessly to purpose becomes creative force: he who knows this is ready to become something higher and stronger than a mere bundle of wavering thoughts and fluctuating sensations; he who does this has become the conscious and intelligent wielder of his mental powers.

THE THOUGHT-FACTOR IN ACHIEVEMENT

ALL that a man achieves and all that he fails to achieve is the direct result of his own thoughts. In a justly ordered universe, where loss of equipoise would mean total destruction, individual responsibility must be absolute. A man's weakness and strength, purity and impurity, are his own, and not another man's; they are brought about by himself, and not by another; and they can only be altered by himself, never by another. His condition is also his own, and not another man's. His suffering and his happiness are evolved from within. As he thinks, so he is; as he continues to think, so he remains.

A strong man cannot help a weaker unless that weaker is willing to be helped, and even then the weak man must become strong of himself; he must, by his own efforts, develop the strength which he admires in another. None but himself can alter his condition.

It has been usual for men to think and to say, "Many men are slaves because one is an oppressor; let us hate the oppressor." Now, however, there is amongst an increasing few a tendency to reverse this judgment, and to say, "One man is an oppressor because many are slaves; let us despise the slaves."

The truth is that oppressor and slave are co-operators in ignorance, and, while seeming to afflict each other, are in reality afflicting themselves. A perfect Knowledge perceives the action of law in the weakness of the oppressed and the misapplied power of the oppressor; a perfect Love, seeing the suffering, which both states entail, condemns neither; a perfect Compassion embraces both oppressor and oppressed.

He who has conquered weakness, and has put away all selfish thoughts, belongs neither to oppressor nor oppressed. He is free.

A man can only rise, conquer, and achieve by lifting up his thoughts. He can only remain weak, and abject, and miserable by refusing to lift up his thoughts.

Before a man can achieve anything, even in worldly things, he must lift his thoughts above slavish animal indulgence. He may not, in order to succeed, give up all animality and selfishness, by any means; but a portion of it must, at least, be sacrificed. A man whose first thought is bestial indulgence could neither think clearly nor plan methodically; he could not find and develop his latent resources, and would fail in any undertaking. Not having commenced to manfully control his thoughts, he is not in a position to control affairs and to adopt serious responsibilities. He is not fit to act independently and stand alone. But he is limited only by the thoughts, which he chooses.

There can be no progress, no achievement without sacrifice, and a man's worldly success will be in the measure that he sacrifices his confused animal thoughts, and fixes his mind on the development of his plans, and the strengthening of his resolution and self-reliance. And the higher he lifts his thoughts, the more manly, upright, and righteous he becomes, the greater will be his success, the more blessed and enduring will be his achievements.

The universe does not favour the greedy, the dishonest, the vicious, although on the mere surface it may sometimes appear to do so; it helps the honest, the magnanimous, the virtuous. All the great Teachers of the ages have declared this in varying forms, and to prove and know it a man has but to persist in making himself more and more virtuous by lifting up his thoughts.

Intellectual achievements are the result of thought consecrated to the search for knowledge, or for the beautiful and true in life and nature. Such achievements may be sometimes connected with vanity and ambition, but they are not the outcome of those characteristics; they are the natural outgrowth of long and arduous effort, and of pure and unselfish thoughts.

Spiritual achievements are the consummation of holy aspirations. He who lives constantly in the conception of noble and lofty thoughts, who dwells upon all that is pure and unselfish, will, as surely as the sun reaches its zenith and the moon its full, become wise and noble in character, and rise into a position of influence and blessedness.

Achievement, of whatever kind, is the crown of effort, the diadem of thought. By the aid of self-control, resolution, purity, righteousness, and well-directed thought a man ascends; by the aid of animality, indolence, impurity, corruption, and confusion of thought a man descends.

A man may rise to high success in the world, and even to lofty altitudes in the spiritual realm, and again descend into weakness and wretchedness by allowing arrogant, selfish, and corrupt thoughts to take possession of him.

Victories attained by right thought can only be maintained by watchfulness. Many give way when success is assured, and rapidly fall back into failure.

All achievements, whether in the business, intellectual, or spiritual world, are the result of definitely directed thought, are governed by the same law and are of the same method; the only difference lies in the object of attainment.

He who would accomplish little must sacrifice little; he who would achieve much must sacrifice much; he who would attain highly must sacrifice greatly.

VISIONS AND IDEALS

THE dreamers are the saviours of the world. As the visible world is sustained by the invisible, so men, through all their trials and sins and sordid vocations, are nourished by the beautiful visions of their solitary dreamers. Humanity cannot forget its dreamers; it cannot let their ideals fade and die; it lives in them; it knows them as the realities which it shall one day see and know.

Composer, sculptor, painter, poet, prophet, sage, these are the makers of the after-world, the architects of heaven. The world is beautiful because they have lived; without them, labouring humanity would perish.

He who cherishes a beautiful vision, a lofty ideal in his heart, will one day realize it. Columbus cherished a vision of another world, and he discovered it; Copernicus fostered the vision of a multiplicity of worlds and a wider universe, and he revealed it; Buddha beheld the vision of a spiritual world of stainless beauty and perfect peace, and he entered into it.

Cherish your visions; cherish your ideals; cherish the music that stirs in your heart, the beauty that forms in your mind, the loveliness that drapes your purest thoughts, for out of them will grow all delightful conditions, all, heavenly environment; of these, if you but remain true to them, your world will at last be built.

To desire is to obtain; to aspire is to, achieve. Shall man's basest desires receive the fullest measure of gratification, and his purest aspirations starve for lack of sustenance? Such is not the Law: such a condition of things can never obtain: "ask and receive."

Dream lofty dreams, and as you dream, so shall you become. Your Vision is the promise of what you shall one day be; your Ideal is the prophecy of what you shall at last unveil.

The greatest achievement was at first and for a time a dream. The oak sleeps in the acorn; the bird waits in the egg; and in the highest vision of the soul a waking angel stirs. Dreams are the seedlings of realities.

Your circumstances may be uncongenial, but they shall not long remain so if you but perceive an Ideal and strive to reach it. You cannot travel within and stand still without. Here is a youth hard pressed by poverty and labour; confined long hours in an unhealthy workshop; unschooled, and lacking all the arts of refinement. But he dreams of better things; he thinks of intelligence, of refinement, of grace and beauty. He conceives of, mentally builds up, an ideal condition of life; the vision of a wider liberty and a larger scope takes possession of him; unrest urges him to action, and he utilizes all his spare time and means, small though they are, to the development of his latent powers and resources. Very soon so altered has his mind become that the workshop can no longer hold him. It has become so out of harmony with his mentality that it falls out of his life as a garment is cast aside, and, with the growth of opportunities, which fit the scope of his expanding powers, he passes out of it forever. Years later we see this youth as a full-grown man. We find him a master of certain forces of the mind, which he wields with worldwide influence and almost unequalled power. In his hands he holds the cords of gigantic responsibilities; he speaks, and lo, lives are changed; men and women hang upon his words and remould their characters, and, sunlike, he becomes the fixed and luminous centre round which innumerable destinies revolve. He has realized the Vision of his youth. He has become one with his Ideal.

And you, too, youthful reader, will realize the Vision (not the idle wish) of your heart, be it base or beautiful, or a mixture of both, for you will always gravitate toward that which you, secretly, most love. Into your hands will be placed the exact results of your own thoughts; you will receive that which you earn; no more, no less. Whatever your present environment may be, you will fall, remain, or rise with your thoughts, your Vision, your Ideal. You will become as small as your controlling desire; as great as your dominant aspiration: in the beautiful words of Stanton Kirkham Davis, "You may be keeping accounts, and presently you shall walk out of the door that for so long has seemed to you the barrier of your ideals, and shall find yourself before an audience—the pen still behind your ear, the ink stains on your fingers and then and there shall pour out the torrent of your inspiration. You may be driving sheep, and you shall wander to the city-bucolic and open-mouthed; shall wander under the intrepid guidance of the spirit into the studio of the master, and after a time he shall say, 'I have nothing more to teach you.' And now you have become the master, who did so recently dream of great things while driving sheep. You shall lay down the saw and the plane to take upon yourself the regeneration of the world."

The thoughtless, the ignorant, and the indolent, seeing only the apparent effects of things and not the things themselves, talk of luck, of fortune, and chance. Seeing a man grow rich, they say, "How lucky he is!" Observing another become intellectual, they exclaim, "How highly favoured he is!" And noting the saintly character and wide influence of another, they remark, "How chance aids him at every turn!" They do not see the trials and failures and struggles which these men have voluntarily encountered in order to gain their experience; have no knowledge of the sacrifices they have made, of the undaunted efforts they have put forth, of the faith they have exercised, that they might overcome the apparently insurmountable, and realize the Vision of their heart. They do not know the darkness and the heartaches; they only see the light and joy, and call it "luck". They do not see the long and arduous journey, but only behold the pleasant goal, and call it "good fortune," do not understand the process, but only perceive the result, and call it chance.

In all human affairs there are efforts, and there are results, and the strength of the effort is the measure of the result. Chance is not. Gifts, powers, material, intellectual, and spiritual possessions are the fruits of effort; they are thoughts completed, objects accomplished, visions realized.

The Vision that you glorify in your mind, the Ideal that you enthrone in your heart—this you will build your life by, this you will become.

SERENITY

CALMNESS of mind is one of the beautiful jewels of wisdom. It is the result of long and patient effort in self-control. Its presence is an indication of ripened experience, and of a more than ordinary knowledge of the laws and operations of thought.

A man becomes calm in the measure that he understands himself as a thought evolved being, for such knowledge necessitates the understanding of others as the result of thought, and as he develops a right understanding, and sees more and more clearly the internal relations of things by the action of cause and effect he ceases to fuss and fume and worry and grieve, and remains poised, steadfast, serene.

The calm man, having learned how to govern himself, knows how to adapt himself to others; and they, in turn, reverence his spiritual strength, and feel that they can learn of him and rely upon him. The more tranquil a man becomes, the greater is his success, his influence, his power for good. Even the ordinary trader will find his business prosperity increase as he develops a greater self-control and equanimity, for people will always prefer to deal with a man whose demeanour is strongly equable.

The strong, calm man is always loved and revered. He is like a shade-giving tree in a thirsty land, or a sheltering rock in a storm. "Who does not love a tranquil heart, a sweet-tempered, balanced life? It does not matter whether it rains or shines, or what changes come to those possessing these blessings, for they are always sweet, serene, and calm. That exquisite poise of character, which we call serenity is the last lesson of culture, the fruitage of the soul. It is precious as wisdom, more to be desired than gold—yea, than even fine gold. How insignificant mere money seeking looks in comparison with a serene life—a life that dwells in the ocean of Truth, beneath the waves, beyond the reach of tempests, in the Eternal Calm!

"How many people we know who sour their lives, who ruin all that is sweet and beautiful by explosive tempers, who destroy their poise of character, and make bad blood! It is a question whether the great majority of people do not ruin their lives and mar their happiness by lack of self-control. How few people we meet in life who are well balanced, who have that exquisite poise which is characteristic of the finished character!

Yes, humanity surges with uncontrolled passion, is tumultuous with ungoverned grief, is blown about by anxiety and doubt only the wise man, only he whose thoughts are controlled and purified, makes the winds and the storms of the soul obey him.

Tempest-tossed souls, wherever ye may be, under whatsoever conditions ye may live, know this in the ocean of life the isles of Blessedness are smiling, and the sunny shore of your ideal awaits your coming. Keep your hand firmly upon the helm of thought. In the bark of your soul reclines the commanding Master; He does but sleep: wake Him. Self-control is strength; Right Thought is mastery; Calmness is power. Say unto your heart, "Peace, be still!"

BIOGRAPHY

James Allen was born on November 28, 1864 in Leicester, England. In 1879, in an effort to support his family and help his failed stocking knitting business, Allen's father traveled to the United States in search of ways to help his business and possibly settle there. Ill-fatedly, he was most likely murdered before his family could join him.

Because his family was under financial duress, James Allen left school and started working to earn money. He first worked as a framework knitter as his father had done. He then went on to become a private secretary until he retired.

In May 1895, James Allen married Lily Louisa Oram in Somerset, England. They had one daughter named Nora on September 10, 1896.

James Allen retired in 1903 and he devoted the remainder of his life to writing. He wrote a total of 19 books, most of which were written after he retired from working.

James Allen settled in Ilfracombe, England and had a routine that allowed to meditate and ponder. After arising each morning, he walked up the Cairn, which was a spot close to his house that overlooked the sea and sat and meditated for about an hour. He'd then return home and write until noon. Afterward, he'd spend time in his garden, spend time with his family, and spend time with his friends.

James Allen was influenced by different writers, such as Milton, Shakespeare, Tolstoy, Emerson, Buddha, and Whitman. And although he grew up Methodist, he was also influenced by other religions such as Buddhism, Taoism, and Protestantism.

He died January 24, 1912. At his funeral, his brother Thomas, scattered James' ashes into the wind, and said "As these ashes of James Allen are cast to the four winds of Heaven, so may the Truth he taught permeate to the four corners of the earth, carrying with it Joy, Peace, and Consolation."

Chronological List of James Allen Books

From Poverty to Power; or, The Realization of Prosperity and Peace (1901) - Contains The Path to Prosperity and The Way of Peace

All These Things Added (1903)

As a Man Thinketh (1903)

Through the Gate of Good; or, Christ and Conduct (1903)

Byways of Blessedness (1904)

Out from the Heart (1904)

Poems of Peace, including the lyrical-dramatic poem Eolaus (1907)

The Life Triumphant: Mastering the Heart and Mind (1908)

Morning and Evening Thoughts (1909)

The Mastery of Destiny (1909)

Above Life's Turmoil (1910)

From Passion to Peace (1910)

Eight Pillars of Prosperity (1911)

Man: King of Mind, Body and Circumstance (1911) Traduit en Français

Light on Life's Difficulties (1912)

Foundation Stones to Happiness and Success (1913)

James Allen's Book of Meditations for Every Day in the Year (1913) - Collection of earlier texts, compiled by his wife Lily L. Allen

Meditations; A Year Book (1913)

Men and Systems (1914)

The Shining Gateway (1915)

The Divine Companion (1919)

Printed in Great Britain
by Amazon

25797275R00020

The Minister's Black Veil

Nathaniel Hawthorne

ISBN-13: 978-1514681312

ISBN-10: 1514681315

The sexton stood in the porch of Milford meeting-house, pulling busily at the bell-rope. The old people of the village came stooping along the street. Children, with bright faces, tripped merrily beside their parents, or mimicked a graver gait, in the conscious dignity of their Sunday clothes. Spruce bachelors looked sidelong at the pretty maidens, and fancied that the Sabbath sunshine made them prettier than on week days. When the throng had mostly streamed into the porch, the sexton began to toll the bell, keeping his eye on the Reverend Mr. Hooper's door. The first glimpse of the clergyman's figure was the signal for the bell to cease its summons.

"But what has good Parson Hooper got upon his face?" cried the sexton in astonishment.

All within hearing immediately turned about, and beheld the semblance of Mr. Hooper, pacing slowly his meditative way towards the meetinghouse. With one accord they started, expressing more wonder than if some strange minister were coming to dust the cushions of Mr. Hooper's pulpit.

"Are you sure it is our parson?" inquired Goodman Gray of the sexton.

"Of a certainty it is good Mr. Hooper," replied the sexton. "He was to have exchanged pulpits with Parson Shute, of Westbury; but Parson Shute sent to excuse himself yesterday, being to preach a funeral sermon."

The cause of so much amazement may appear sufficiently slight. Mr. Hooper, a gentlemanly person, of about thirty, though still a bachelor, was dressed with due clerical neatness, as if a careful wife had starched his band, and brushed the weekly dust from his Sunday's garb. There was but one thing remarkable in his appearance. Swathed about his forehead, and hanging down over his face, so low as to be shaken by his breath, Mr. Hooper had on a black veil. On a nearer view it seemed to consist of two folds of crape, which entirely concealed his features, except the mouth and chin, but probably did not intercept his sight, further than to give a darkened aspect to all living and inanimate things. With this gloomy shade before him, good Mr. Hooper walked onward, at a slow and quiet pace, stooping somewhat, and looking on the ground, as is customary with abstracted men, yet nodding kindly to those of his parishioners who still waited on the meeting-house steps. But so wonder-struck were they that his greeting hardly met with a return.

"I can't really feel as if good Mr. Hooper's face was behind that piece of crape," said the sexton.

"I don't like it," muttered an old woman, as she hobbled into the meeting-house. "He has changed himself into something awful, only by hiding his face."

"Our parson has gone mad!" cried Goodman

Gray, following him across the threshold.

A rumor of some unaccountable phenomenon had preceded Mr. Hooper into the meeting-house, and set all the congregation astir. Few could refrain from twisting their heads towards the door; many stood upright, and turned directly about; while several little boys clambered upon the seats, and came down again with a terrible racket. There was a general bustle, a rustling of the women's gowns and shuffling of the men's feet, greatly at variance with that hushed repose which should attend the entrance of the minister. But Mr. Hooper appeared not to notice the perturbation of his people. He entered with an almost noiseless step, bent his head mildly to the pews on each side, and bowed as he passed his oldest parishioner, a white-haired great grandsire, who occupied an arm-chair in the centre of the aisle. It was strange to observe how slowly this venerable man became conscious of something singular in the appearance of his pastor. He seemed not fully to partake of the prevailing wonder, till Mr. Hooper had ascended the stairs, and showed himself in the pulpit, face to face with his congregation, except for the black veil. That mysterious emblem was never once withdrawn. It shook with his measured breath, as he gave out the psalm; it threw its obscurity between him and the holy page, as he read the Scriptures; and while he prayed, the veil lay heavily on his uplifted countenance. Did he seek to hide it from the dread Being whom he was addressing?

Such was the effect of this simple piece of crape, that more than one woman of delicate nerves was forced to leave the meeting-house. Yet perhaps the pale-faced congregation was almost as fearful a sight to the minister, as his black veil to them.

Mr. Hooper had the reputation of a good preacher, but not an energetic one: he strove to win his people heavenward by mild, persuasive influences, rather than to drive them thither by the thunders of the Word. The sermon which he now delivered was marked by the same characteristics of style and manner as the general series of his pulpit oratory. But there was something, either in the sentiment of the discourse itself, or in the imagination of the auditors, which made it greatly the most powerful effort that they had ever heard from their pastor's lips. It was tinged, rather more darkly than usual, with the gentle gloom of Mr. Hooper's temperament. The subject had reference to secret sin, and those sad mysteries which we hide from our nearest and dearest, and would fain conceal from our own consciousness, even forgetting that the Omniscient can detect them. A subtle power was breathed into his words. Each member of the congregation, the most innocent girl, and the man of hardened breast, felt as if the preacher had crept upon them, behind his awful

Pathos = a quality that evokes pity & sadness.

veil, and discovered their hoarded iniquity of deed or thought. Many spread their clasped hands on their bosoms. There was nothing terrible in what Mr. Hooper said, at least, no violence; and yet, with every tremor of his melancholy voice, the hearers quaked. An unsought pathos came hand in hand with awe. So sensible were the audience of some unwonted attribute in their minister, that they longed for a breath of wind to blow aside the veil, almost believing that a stranger's visage would be discovered, though the form, gesture, and voice were those of Mr. Hooper.

At the close of the services, the people hurried out with indecorous confusion, eager to communicate their pent-up amazement, and conscious of lighter spirits the moment they lost sight of the black veil. Some gathered in little circles, huddled closely together, with their mouths all whispering in the centre; some went homeward alone, wrapt in silent meditation; some talked loudly, and profaned the Sabbath day with ostentatious laughter. A few shook their sagacious heads, intimating that they could penetrate the mystery; while one or two affirmed that there was no mystery at all, but only that Mr. Hooper's eyes were so weakened by the midnight lamp, as to require a shade. After a brief interval, forth came good Mr. Hooper also, in the rear of his flock. Turning his veiled face from one group to another, he paid due reverence to the hoary heads, saluted the middle aged with kind dignity as their friend and spiritual guide, greeted the young with mingled authority and love, and laid his hands on the little children's heads to bless them. Such was always his custom on the Sabbath day. Strange and bewildered looks repaid him for his courtesy. None, as on former occasions, aspired to the honor of walking by their pastor's side. Old Squire Saunders, doubtless by an accidental lapse of memory, neglected to invite Mr. Hooper to his table, where the good clergyman had been wont to bless the food, almost every Sunday since his settlement. He returned, therefore, to the parsonage, and, at the moment of closing the door, was observed to look back upon the people, all of whom had their eyes fixed upon the minister. A sad smile gleamed faintly from beneath the black veil, and flickered about his mouth, glimmering as he disappeared.

"How strange," said a lady, "that a simple black veil, such as any woman might wear on her bonnet, should become such a terrible thing on Mr. Hooper's face!"

"Something must surely be amiss with Mr. Hooper's intellects," observed her husband, the physician of the village. "But the strangest part of the affair is the effect of this vagary, even on a sober-minded man like myself. The black veil, though it covers only our pastor's face, throws its influence over his whole person, and makes him ghostlike from head to foot. Do you not feel it so?"

"Truly do I," replied the lady; "and I would not be alone with him for the world. I wonder he is not afraid to be alone with himself!"

"Men sometimes are so," said her husband.

The afternoon service was attended with similar circumstances. At its conclusion, the bell tolled for the funeral of a young lady. The relatives and friends were assembled in the house, and the more distant acquaintances stood about the door, speaking of the good qualities of the deceased, when their talk was interrupted by the appearance of Mr. Hooper, still covered with his black veil. It was now an appropriate emblem. The clergyman stepped into the room where the corpse was laid, and bent over the coffin, to take a last farewell of his deceased parishioner. As he stooped, the veil hung straight down from his forehead, so that, if her eyelids had not been closed forever, the dead maiden might have seen his face. Could Mr. Hooper be fearful of her glance, that he so hastily caught back the black veil? A person who watched the interview between the dead and living, scrupled not to affirm, that, at the instant when the clergyman's features were disclosed, the corpse had slightly shuddered, rustling the shroud and muslin cap, though the countenance retained the composure of death. A superstitious old woman

Wedding to a funeral quick

important page

was the only witness of this prodigy. From the coffin Mr. Hooper passed into the chamber of the mourners, and thence to the head of the staircase, to make the funeral prayer. It was a tender and heart-dissolving prayer, full of sorrow, yet so imbued with celestial hopes, that the music of a heavenly harp, swept by the fingers of the dead, seemed faintly to be heard among the saddest accents of the minister. The people trembled, though they but darkly understood him when he prayed that they, and himself, and all of mortal race, might be ready, as he trusted this young maiden had been, for the dreadful hour that should snatch the veil from their faces. The bearers went heavily forth, and the mourners followed, saddening all the street, with the dead before them, and Mr. Hooper in his black veil behind.

"Why do you look back?" said one in the procession to his partner.

"I had a fancy," replied she, "that the minister and the maiden's spirit were walking hand in hand."

"And so had I, at the same moment," said the other.

That night, the handsomest couple in Milford village were to be joined in wedlock. Though reckoned a melancholy man, Mr. Hooper had a placid cheerfulness for such occasions, which often excited a sympathetic smile where livelier merriment would have been thrown away. There was no quality of his disposition which made him more beloved than this. The company at the wedding awaited his arrival with impatience, trusting that the strange awe, which had gathered over him throughout the day, would now be dispelled. But such was not the result. When Mr. Hooper came, the first thing that their eyes rested on was the same horrible black veil, which had added deeper gloom to the funeral, and could portend nothing but evil to the wedding. Such was its immediate effect on the guests that a cloud seemed to have rolled duskily from beneath the black crape, and dimmed the light of the candles. The bridal pair stood up before the minister. But the bride's cold fingers quivered in the tremulous hand of the bridegroom, and her deathlike paleness caused a whisper that the maiden who had been buried a few hours before was come from her grave to be married. If ever another wedding were so dismal, it was that famous one where they tolled the wedding knell. After performing the ceremony, Mr. Hooper raised a glass of wine to his lips, wishing happiness to the newmarried couple in a strain of mild pleasantry that ought to have brightened the features of the guests, like a cheerful gleam from the hearth. At that instant, catching a glimpse of his figure in the looking-glass, the black veil involved his own spirit in the horror with which it overwhelmed all others. His frame shuddered, his lips grew white, he spilt the untasted wine upon the carpet, and rushed forth into the darkness. For the Earth, too, had on her Black Veil.

The next day, the whole village of Milford talked of little else than Parson Hooper's black veil. That, and the mystery concealed behind it, supplied a topic for discussion between acquaintances meeting in the street, and good women gossiping at their open windows. It was the first item of news that the tavern-keeper told to his guests. The children babbled of it on their way to school. One imitative little imp covered his face with an old black handkerchief, thereby so affrighting his playmates that the panic seized himself, and he well-nigh lost his wits by his own waggery.

It was remarkable that all of the busybodies and impertinent people in the parish, not one ventured to put the plain question to Mr. Hooper, wherefore he did this thing. Hitherto, whenever there appeared the slightest call for such interference, he had never lacked advisers, nor shown himself averse to be guided by their judgment. If he erred at all, it was by so painful a degree of self-distrust, that even the mildest censure would lead him to consider an indifferent action as a crime. Yet, though so well acquainted with this amiable weakness, no individual among his parishioners chose to make the black veil a subject of friendly remonstrance. There was a feeling of dread, neither plainly confessed nor carefully concealed, which caused each to shift the responsibility upon another, till at length it was found expedient to send a deputation of the church, in order to deal with Mr. Hooper about the mystery, before it should grow into a scandal. Never did an embassy so ill discharge its duties. The minister received then with friendly courtesy, but became silent, after they were seated, leaving to his visitors the whole burden of introducing their important business. The topic, it might be supposed, was obvious enough. There was the black veil swathed round Mr. Hooper's forehead, and concealing every feature above his placid mouth, on which, at times, they could perceive the glimmering of a melancholy smile. But that piece of crape, to their imagination, seemed to hang down before his heart, the symbol of a fearful secret between him and them. Were the veil but cast aside, they might speak freely of it, but not till then. Thus they sat a considerable time, speechless, confused, and shrinking uneasily from Mr. Hooper's eye, which they felt to be fixed upon them with an invisible glance. Finally, the deputies returned abashed to their constituents, pronouncing the matter too weighty to be handled, except by a council of the churches, if, indeed, it might not require a general synod.

But there was one person in the village unappalled by the awe with which the black veil had impressed all beside herself. When the deputies returned without an explanation, or even venturing to demand one, she, with the calm energy of her character, determined to chase away the strange cloud that appeared to be settling round Mr. Hooper, every moment more darkly than before. As his plighted wife, it should be her privilege to know what the black veil concealed. At the minister's first visit, therefore, she entered upon the subject with a direct simplicity, which made the task easier both for him and her. After he had seated himself, she fixed her eyes steadfastly upon the veil, but could discern nothing of the dreadful gloom that had so overawed the multitude: it was but a double fold of crape, hanging down from his forehead to his mouth, and slightly stirring with his breath.

"No," said she aloud, and smiling, "there is nothing terrible in this piece of crape, except that it hides a face which I am always glad to look upon. Come, good sir, let the sun shine from behind the cloud. First lay aside your black veil: then tell me why you put it on."

Mr. Hooper's smile glimmered faintly.

"There is an hour to come," said he, "when all of us shall cast aside our veils. Take it not amiss, beloved friend, if I wear this piece of crape till then."

"Your words are a mystery, too," returned the young lady. "Take away the veil from them, at least."

"Elizabeth, I will," said he, "so far as my vow may suffer me. Know, then, this veil is a type and a symbol, and I am bound to wear it ever, both in light and darkness, in solitude and before the gaze of multitudes, and as with strangers, so with my familiar friends. No mortal eye will see it withdrawn. This dismal shade must separate me from the world: even you, Elizabeth, can never come behind it!"

"What grievous affliction hath befallen you," she earnestly inquired, "that you should thus darken your eyes forever?"

"If it be a sign of mourning," replied Mr. Hooper, "I, perhaps, like most other mortals, have sorrows dark enough to be typified by a black veil."

"But what if the world will not believe that it is the type of an innocent sorrow?" urged Elizabeth. "Beloved and respected as you are, there may be whispers that you hide your face under the consciousness of secret sin. For the sake of your holy office, do away this scandal!"

The color rose into her cheeks as she intimated the nature of the rumors that were already abroad in the village. But Mr. Hooper's mildness did not forsake him. He even smiled again—that same sad smile, which always appeared like a faint glimmering of light, proceeding from the obscurity beneath the veil.

"If I hide my face for sorrow, there is cause enough," he merely replied; "and if I cover it for secret sin, what mortal might not do the same?"

And with this gentle, but unconquerable obstinacy did he resist all her entreaties. At length Elizabeth sat silent. For a few moments she appeared lost in thought, considering, probably, what new methods might be tried to withdraw her lover from so dark a fantasy, which, if it had no other meaning, was perhaps a symptom of mental disease. Though of a firmer character than his own, the tears rolled down her cheeks. But, in an instant, as it were, a new feeling took the place of sorrow: her eyes were fixed insensibly on the black veil, when, like a sudden twilight in the air, its terrors fell around her. She arose, and stood trembling before him.

"And do you feel it then, at last?" said he mournfully.

She made no reply, but covered her eyes with her hand, and turned to leave the room. He rushed forward and caught her arm.

"Have patience with me, Elizabeth!" cried he, passionately. "Do not desert me, though this veil must be between us here on earth. Be mine, and hereafter there shall be no veil over my face, no darkness between our souls! It is but a mortal veil—it is not for eternity! O! you know not how lonely I am, and how frightened, to be alone behind my black veil. Do not leave me in this miserable obscurity forever!"

"Lift the veil but once, and look me in the face," said she.

"Never! It cannot be!" replied Mr. Hooper.

"Then farewell!" said Elizabeth.

She withdrew her arm from his grasp, and slowly departed, pausing at the door, to give one long shuddering gaze, that s
the mystery of the blac
grief, Mr. Hooper sm
material emblem had sep
though the horrors, whi
be drawn darkly betweer

→ the idea of the Self being haunted
→ him hiding is a Spiritual power
→ External representation of Secrets
p. 15

From that time no attempts were made to remove Mr. Hooper's black veil, or, by a direct appeal, to discover the secret which it was supposed to hide. By persons who claimed a superiority to popular prejudice, it was reckoned merely an eccentric whim, such as often mingles with the sober actions of men otherwise rational, and tinges them all with its own semblance of insanity. But with the multitude, good Mr. Hooper was irreparbly a bugbear. He could not walk the street with any peace of mind, so conscious was he that the gentle and timid would turn aside to avoid him, and that others would make it a point of hardihood to throw themselves in his way. The impertinence of the latter class compelled him to give up his customary

Does the veil represent a distorted view on reality?

Not a tale of terror but a tale of horror covered in a veil? p. 16

al ground; for when he gate, there would always be faces behind the gravestones, peeping at his black veil. A fable went the rounds that the stare of the dead people drove him thence. It grieved him, to the very depth of his kind heart, to observe how the children fled from his approach, breaking up their merriest sports, while his melancholy figure was yet afar off. Their instinctive dread caused him to feel more strongly than aught else, that a preternatural horror was interwoven with the threads of the black crape. In truth, his own antipathy to the veil was known to be so great, that he never willingly passed before a mirror, nor stooped to drink at a still fountain, lest, in its peaceful bosom, he should be affrighted by himself. This was what gave plausibility to the whispers, that Mr. Hooper's conscience tortured him for some great crime too horrible to be entirely concealed, or otherwise than so obscurely intimated. Thus, from beneath the black veil, there rolled a cloud into the sunshine, an ambiguity of sin or sorrow, which enveloped the poor minister, so that love or sympathy could never reach him. It was said that ghost and fiend consorted with him there. With self-shudderings and outward terrors, he walked continually in its shadow, groping darkly within his own soul, or gazing through a medium that saddened the whole world. Even the lawless wind, it was believed, respected his dreadful secret, and never blew aside the veil. But still good Mr. Hooper sadly smiled at the pale visages of the worldly throng as he passed by.

Among all its bad influences, the black veil had the one desirable effect, of making its wearer a very efficient clergyman. By the aid of his mysterious emblem—for there was no other apparent cause—he became a man of awful power over souls that were in agony for sin. His converts always regarded him with a dread peculiar to themselves, affirming, though but figuratively, that, before he brought them to celestial light, they had been with him behind the black veil. Its gloom, indeed, enabled him to sympathize with all dark affections. Dying sinners cried aloud for Mr. Hooper, and would not yield their breath till he appeared; though ever, as he stooped to whisper consolation, they shuddered at the veiled face so near their own. Such were the terrors of the black veil, even when Death had bared his visage! Strangers came long distances to attend service at his church, with the mere idle purpose of gazing at his figure, because it was forbidden them to behold his face. But many were made to quake ere they departed! Once, during Governor Belcher's administration, Mr. Hooper was appointed to preach the election sermon. Covered with his black veil, he stood before the chief magistrate, the council, and the representatives, and wrought so deep an impression, that the legislative measures of that year were characterized by all the gloom and piety of our earliest ancestral sway.

In this manner Mr. Hooper spent a long life, irreproachable in outward act, yet shrouded in dismal suspicions; kind and loving, though unloved, and dimly feared; a man apart from men, shunned in their health and joy, but ever summoned to their aid in mortal anguish. As years wore on, shedding their snows above his sable veil, he acquired a name throughout the New England churches, and they called him Father Hooper. Nearly all his parishioners, who were of mature age when he was settled, had been borne away by many a funeral: he had one congregation in the church, and a more crowded one in the churchyard; and having wrought so late into the evening, and done his work so well, it was now good Father Hooper's turn to rest.

Several persons were visible by the shaded candlelight, in the death chamber of the old clergyman. Natural connections he had none. But there was the decorously grave, though unmoved physician, seeking only to mitigate the last pangs of the patient whom he could not save. There were the deacons, and other eminently pious members of his church. There, also, was the Reverend Mr. Clark, of Westbury, a young and zealous divine, who had ridden in haste to pray by the bedside of the expiring minister. There was the nurse, no hired handmaiden of death, but one whose calm affection had endured thus long in secrecy, in solitude, amid the chill of age, and would not perish, even at the dying hour. Who, but Elizabeth! And there lay the hoary head of good Father Hooper upon the death pillow, with the black veil still swathed about his brow, and reaching down over his face, so that each more difficult gasp of his faint breath caused it to stir. All through life that piece of crape had hung between him and the world: it had separated him from cheerful brotherhood and woman's love, and kept him in that saddest of all prisons, his own heart; and still it lay upon his face, as if to deepen the gloom of his darksome chamber, and shade him from the sunshine of eternity.

For some time previous, his mind had been confused, wavering doubtfully between the past and the present, and hovering forward, as it were, at intervals, into the indistinctness of the world to come. There had been feverish turns, which tossed him from side to side, and wore away what little strength he had. But in his most convulsive struggles, and in the wildest vagaries of his intellect, when no other thought retained its sober influence, he still showed an awful solicitude lest the black veil should slip aside.* Even if his bewildered soul could have forgotten, there was a faithful woman at this pillow, who, with averted eyes, would have covered

KEY QUOTE

even when he was ill she stayed

that aged face, which she had last beheld in the comeliness of manhood. At length the death-stricken old man lay quietly in the torpor of mental and bodily exhaustion, with an imperceptible pulse, and breath that grew fainter and fainter, except when a long, deep, and irregular inspiration seemed to prelude the flight of his spirit.

The minister of Westbury approached the bedside.

"Venerable Father Hooper," said he, "the moment of your release is at hand. Are you ready for the lifting of the veil that shuts in time from eternity?"

Father Hooper at first replied merely by a feeble motion of his head; then, apprehensive, perhaps, that his meaning might be doubted, he exerted himself to speak.

"Yea," said he, in faint accents, "my soul hath a patient weariness until that veil be lifted."

"And is it fitting," resumed the Reverend Mr. Clark, "that a man so given to prayer, of such a blameless example, holy in deed and thought, so far as mortal judgment may pronounce; is it fitting that a father in the church should leave a shadow on his memory, that may seem to blacken a life so pure? I pray you, my venerable brother, let not this thing be! Suffer us to be gladdened by your triumphant aspect as you go to your reward. Before the veil of eternity be lifted, let me cast aside this black veil from your face!"

And thus speaking, the Reverend Mr. Clark bent forward to reveal the mystery of so many years. But, exerting a sudden energy, that made all the beholders stand aghast, Father Hooper snatched both his hands from beneath the bedclothes, and pressed them strongly on the black veil, resolute to struggle, if the minister of Westbury would contend with a dying man.

"Never!" cried the veiled clergyman. "On earth, never!"

"Dark old man!" exclaimed the affrighted minister, "with what horrible crime upon your soul are you now passing to the judgment?"

Father Hooper's breath heaved; it rattled in his throat; but, with a mighty effort, grasping forward with his hands, he caught hold of life, and held it back till he should speak. He even raised himself in bed; and there he sat, shivering with the arms of death around him, while the black veil hung down, awful, at that last moment, in the gathered terrors of a lifetime. And yet the faint, sad smile, so often there, now seemed to glimmer from its obscurity, and linger on Father Hooper's lips.

"Why do you tremble at me alone?" cried he, turning his veiled face round the circle of pale spectators. "Tremble also at each other! Have men avoided me, and women shown no pity, and children screamed and fled, only for my black veil?

What, but the mystery which it obscurely typifies, has made this piece of crape so awful? When the friend shows his inmost heart to his friend; the lover to his best beloved; when man does not vainly shrink from the eye of his Creator, loathsomely treasuring up the secret of his sin; then deem me a monster, for the symbol beneath which I have lived, and die! I look around me, and, lo! on every visage a Black Veil!"

While his auditors shrank from one another, in mutual affright, Father Hooper fell back upon his pillow, a veiled corpse, with a faint smile lingering on the lips. Still veiled, they laid him in his coffin, and a veiled corpse they bore him to the grave. The grass of many years has sprung up and withered on that grave, the burial stone is moss-grown, and good Mr. Hooper's face is dust; but awful is still the thought that it mouldered beneath the Black Veil!

→ Summary.

- he gets a glimpse of what he looks like and spills his drink
-

Printed in Great Britain
by Amazon

25797200R00020